For Noah:
About time, too.

First published in 2006 in Great Britain by
Barrington Stoke Ltd
www.barringtonstoke.co.uk

ISBN-10: 1-842993-93-3
ISBN-13: 978-1-84299-393-4

Printed in Great Britain by Bell & Bain Ltd

Contents

1 Saturday 15th october   1

2 Sunday 16th october   7

3 Monday 17th october   15

4 Tuesday 18th october   22

5 Wednesday 19th october   31

6 Thursday 20th october   42

7 Friday 21st october   51

Saturday 15ᵗʰ october

Hi, and welcome to my diary. My name is Darren Smith. I'm almost 11 years old and I'm going to be a rock star. I did want to be a footballer, but I don't any more. I changed my mind when I met my new friend's big brother. He's called Nigel. What I mean is, my new friend's big brother's called Nigel, not my new friend. My new friend's called Steven.

Nigel is 14. He's got long hair and a guitar. I think he might have even got a girlfriend. Nigel's going to be a rock star too. He is **SO** cool.

Nigel says there was this band called **Nirvana.** The singer was a guy called **Kurt Cobain.** And he kept a diary. Well, he didn't just *keep* a diary. He wrote in it as well! In the end, the diary got made into a book and loads of people bought it. Maybe my diary will get made into a book too! (So I'd better not swear, or write anything rude. Just in case my mum reads this!)

So anyway, we were all listening to Nirvana – that's me, Steven and Nigel – when Steven and Nigel's dad walked in. I thought he was going to tell Nigel to turn the music down or something. But he didn't. He just stood there and then said, "Smells Like Teen Spirit, eh? Great song!"

I couldn't believe it. Steven and Nigel's dad was really cool! But dads aren't cool. Dads are boring. Well, my dad is. He wants me to call him Colin, by the way. Steven and Nigel's dad, I mean, not my dad. That would be stupid. My dad's called Trevor.

NOT → COOL

← cool

Colin went to see Nirvana playing live! It was in 1991. They'd just released an album called Nevermind. It's got a picture of a bare naked baby swimming underwater on the front of it. (I'm not being rude, by the way, Mum. It really has!) I shouldn't think my dad's ever been to a rock concert in his life. Colin's been to loads. He even met Steven and Nigel's mum at a concert!

It was a concert by a band called XTC. This was like, back in 1980 or something. We're talking ancient history here! Anyway Colin got talking to this girl. She was called Jane. They were both fans of the band. Their favourite song was a song called Making Plans For Nigel. Well, one thing led to another and Colin and Jane ended up getting married. A few years later they had a baby. And guess what? They called him Nigel! Because Making Plans For Nigel was like, their special song or something!

How cool is that? Being named after a song! I wish *I'd* been named after a song. But there aren't any songs with Darren in the title. Not as far as I know, anyway.

5 other songs with boys' names in them

Michael - Franz Ferdinand

St Jimmy - Green Day

Tony's Theme - Pixies

John I'm Only Dancing - David Bowie

Arnold Layne - Pink Floyd

5 songs with
girls' names in them

Polly - Nirvana

Leila - Oasis

Lucy In The Sky With Diamonds
- The Beatles

Come On Eileen
- Dexy's Midnight Runners

Virginia Plain - Roxy Music

Sunday 16ᵗʰ October

Just been round to Steven's house again. Nigel is a *wicked* guitar player! His fingers were going up and down the guitar so fast, they were just a blur! I asked him how long he'd been playing for. He said 20 minutes. I said no, I mean when did you first start playing guitar. Nigel said three years ago.

Three years ago? That means Nigel must have started playing guitar when he was eleven. And I'll be eleven next week! So if I start to play guitar now, maybe I'll be as good as Nigel when I'm his age! Wow! Just think!

There's just one teeny problem. I don't have a guitar.

But, hey, that's OK, because I don't think Mum and Dad have got me my birthday

present yet and it's my birthday next week. Maybe I should start dropping hints? It worked last year with the Man United strip and the Championship Manager game. Perhaps it's too late to drop hints. Perhaps I should just tell them.

You never know. It might work. Mind you, I bet I have to do something in return. It's always the same with my parents. Well, with my dad anyway. He never says, yes of course you can have a new pair of trainers, Darren. It's always, yes of course you can have a new pair of trainers, Darren. *If* you cut the grass, or tidy your room, or do the washing up for the next eighteen years, or something.

But I don't mind. Not if it means I get an electric guitar in the end. Hey, if it means I get an electric guitar, I'll jump through a hoop of fire naked if I have to!

Steven's not very interested in rock music. He's much more into football. That's how we started being friends. He'd only just moved to our school and we were both on the same team one lunch time. He made a goal for me. I made one for him. That was it. We were best mates after that.

Football's all me and Steven ever seem to talk about. It's funny. I didn't even know he had a brother until I went to his house. He'd never said anything about him before. I don't think he knows just how cool Nigel is.

Anyway, guess what? Nigel let me have a go on his guitar! Not that I could play it or anything. But I held it! Nigel said I could strum it if I wanted, so I did. It sounded great. And dead loud. That's because it was plugged into an **amplifier**.

Nigel said that the long bit of the guitar is called the **neck**. The **neck** has lots of lines going across it – they're called **frets**. That's so that you know where to put your fingers. At the end of the neck there are these things called **tuning pegs**. You turn them when you want to tune the **strings** and make them sound right. There are **six strings** on Nigel's guitar, by the way, but some guitars have **twelve** strings. Oh, and under the strings there are these things called **pick-ups**. I think they make the sound electric or something, but I'm not sure.

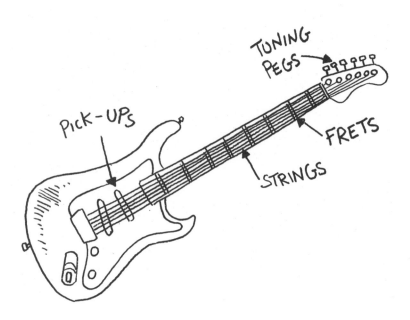

TUNING PEGS

PICK-UPS

FRETS

STRINGS

Nigel showed me how to play something
called a **chord**. That's when you play a few
notes together at the same time. You have
to press down on a few of the strings in
different places. Your fingers make a shape.
The chord I played was called D major. It
felt a bit weird, but it sounded OK. Nigel
said I was a natural! He said I'd be as good
as **Jimi Hendrix** before I knew it! I bet Jimi

Hendrix didn't only know one chord though. I bet he knew loads.

Nigel says that Jimi Hendrix was one of the best guitarists ever. And he didn't just play guitar, he sang and wrote songs as well. He wrote loads of well known songs like Purple Haze, Crosstown Traffic and Voodoo Chile. And guess what? He was so amazing, he could play guitar with his teeth! And behind his back!

Sometimes he even set fire to his guitar on stage! I don't understand that. If I ever get an electric guitar, the last thing I'm going to do is set fire to it!

Some more famous guitarists

Jimmy Page - Led Zeppelin

Keith Richards
- The Rolling Stones

The Edge - U2

Slash - Guns 'n' Roses
and Velvet Revolver

John Frusciante
- Red Hot Chili Peppers

Kirk Hammett - Metallica

Eric Clapton

Brian May - Queen

Pete Townsend - The Who

Angus Young - AC/DC

Monday 17th october

Well, I did it! I told my parents what I wanted for my birthday! I waited till after tea. Mum was doing the washing up as normal. Dad was doing the crossword as normal. I took a deep breath and came right out with it. "Mum and Dad? Guess what I want for my birthday? An electric guitar!"

Dad asked me what I wanted one of those for. So I told him I was going to be a rock star. Mum said, "That's nice, dear."

Dad didn't say anything else. Not just then. He put his newspaper down and took a sip of coffee. I thought, here we go. Any minute now he's going to start droning on about how there were no such things as electric guitars when he was a boy and how he was lucky if he got a bar of chocolate for his birthday. But he didn't. He said he'd think about it. Which was better than saying no anyway.

By the way, there *were* such things as electric guitars when my dad was a boy. My dad's old, but he's not that old! In fact electric guitars have been around since the 1940s. That's amazing! That's when my grandparents were little!

I know all about the history of the electric guitar now. I went upstairs and did a search on the internet. Loads of stuff came up. Some of it was great. Like all the different makes of guitar you can get and stuff.

Fenders and **Gibsons** are the most famous makes of electric guitars. They haven't changed all that much since they were first made!

Fender guitars were invented by this guy called **Leo Fender**. There are two main kinds of Fender electric guitars. One's called a **Fender Telecaster** and the other's a **Fender Stratocaster**. Then there was this guy called **Les Paul**. He invented an electric guitar called the **Gibson Les Paul**. How cool is that? Having a guitar named

FENDER
TELECASTER

GIBSON
LES PAUL

FENDER
STRATOCASTER

after you? Maybe one day there'll be a type of guitar called the Gibson Darren Smith!

Anyway, after I'd been on the internet for a while, Dad called me downstairs again. He said that he'd had a think. I was like, come on then Dad! Spit it out! Can I have an electric guitar or not? (I didn't say that of course. But I thought it!)

Dad didn't say anything for ages. It was like The X Factor, or one of those other TV shows. You know, when the presenter says "The person leaving the show tonight is ..." and then doesn't say anything for about a week! It drives you mad!

Then, at last, he said it. The words I'd longed to hear. Yes, I *could* have an electric guitar! I looked at Dad. Dad looked at me. I didn't dare smile. I had a funny feeling Dad hadn't finished. And he hadn't. He still had three more words to say. Three more words I *hadn't* longed to hear. "On one condition."

Aaaaaaaagh!!! I told you, didn't I?
There's always *one condition*! You know,
something I have to do? There always is!

And what is that condition, Darren? I
hear you ask. Well, I'll tell you. Between

now and my birthday, Dad's going to give
me three clues. And if I can work out those
clues I get an electric guitar!

That's the bad news.

The *good* news is that the clues are all
going to have something to do with rock
music. Which is brilliant, because I can just
look stuff up on the internet! And if it's not

on the internet? I'll ask Nigel! Nigel knows everything about rock!

My Top 10 guitar makes

1. Fender

2. Gibson

3. Epiphone

4. Gretsch

5. Ibanez

6. Rickenbacker

7. Vintage

8. Squier

9. Stagg

10. BC Rich

Tuesday 18th october

Dad gave me my first clue today. He wrote it on a bit of paper and put it on the kitchen table. It was there waiting for me when I went down to breakfast.

"A singer of a well known rock band who sounds like a northern English city?"

I looked hard at the clue for a long time. I didn't understand it. There are so many different rock bands. And so many cities!

And anyway I'm rubbish at crossword clues. It's all right for Dad. He does his stupid crossword every day. I never do crosswords. I'm rubbish at them!

I began to think that maybe getting my guitar wasn't going to be that easy after all. My dream of being a rock star was fading fast. I'd be lucky to get an electric guitar for my *next* birthday, never mind this one!

Just then there was a knock at the door. It was Steven. He'd come round to see if I fancied a kick about. We're on half-term. That's why there's no school at the moment.

I was really glad to see Steven, even if I don't like football any more. Well, I mean I do like football. Just not as much as before, that's all. But I didn't say anything. I didn't want to upset Steven. And anyway it gave me something else to think about. You know, instead of working out stupid clues and stuff.

So anyway, we played football for a while and it was great. I was Man United. Steven was Chelsea. Chelsea won 37-21, but I didn't care.

Then Steven asked me if I wanted to go round to his house. I asked him if Nigel was there. Steven said yes he was. So I said OK, in that case I'd go round. Steven gave me this look. I think I might have upset him after all. I didn't mean to, but I think I did.

As soon as we walked through the door I could hear music. It was coming from Nigel's room. It was hard to describe. The music I mean, not Nigel's room. Nigel's room is easy to describe. It's dead cool. The walls are covered in posters of bands and rock stars.

There's a poster of Jimi Hendrix and there's one of Kurt Cobain. And there's one of this band called **The White Stripes**. There's only two people in **The White Stripes**. Nigel says that they're called **Jack** and **Meg White**. He says that they come from Detroit in the USA and that they've got this song called *Seven Nation Army*. Nigel can play it on his guitar. It's awesome!

The music I could hear coming from Nigel's room had loud bits and soft bits, like Nirvana's music does. But the singer sounded nothing like Kurt Cobain. Kurt

Cobain had a gritty sort of voice. Like he gargled with a bucket full of gravel every morning or something. The guy singing this music had a much smoother kind of voice. And he was singing really high. Like a grown-up choir boy or something.

When Nigel came down, I asked him what the name of the band was. He said they were called **Radiohead** and that the album was called *OK Computer*. I said that's a cool name for an album. Nigel said I could borrow it if I wanted. So I did.

I listened to it as soon as I got home. It's great. It's got songs with names like *Karma Police* and *No Surprises* on it. But my favourite is this really mad song called *Paranoid Android*. It's dead long and complicated. Well, it sounds complicated to me!

Anyway, there's this kind of little booklet thing that comes with the CD. It's got all these weird pictures in it and the words to the songs and stuff. I started to read it. And guess what I found out? The singer of Radiohead is called **Thom Yorke**!

Thom *Yorke*! Do you get it? "A singer of a band who sounds like a northern English city?" Well, York is a city in the north of England! OK, so it's not spelt quite the same. But it *sounds* like a northern English city!

I rushed downstairs and told Dad. He said is that your final answer? You know, like they do on Who Wants To Be A Millionaire? So I said yeah. He said do you want to phone a friend? I said no. So then he looked at me and did one of those great big long pauses. Then guess what? He said I was right!

Yeah! Rock stardom here I come!

Some stuff about Radiohead

They got together in Oxford, in 1986. They used to be called 'On A Friday' because that's the day they practised.

***

There are two brothers in Radiohead. Their names are Colin and Jonny Greenwood.

***

The full line-up is Thom Yorke - vocals and guitar; Jonny Greenwood - guitar; Ed O'Brien - guitar; Colin Greenwood - bass; Phil Selway - drums.

***

One of Thom Yorke's best friends is Michael Stipe. Michael Stipe is the singer in a band called R.E.M. (But R.E.M. aren't from Oxford. They're from Athens. Not Athens in Greece. Athens in Georgia, USA!)

***

Jonny Greenwood and Phil Selway both appear in Harry Potter And The Goblet Of Fire! Not the book. The movie!

Wednesday 19th October

When I came down to breakfast this morning the next clue was waiting for me.

"Could this charming band from Manchester be distant cousins?"

I read the clue over and over again, but I still didn't get it. What on earth was he on about now? This charming band? Distant cousins? From Manchester? We don't have any cousins in Manchester! I wish we did, because then we could visit them and I could go and watch Man United!

After a while, Dad came and sat down next to me. He asked how I was getting on with clue number two. I told him that I wasn't! Big mistake! Dad started going on and on about not giving up and how you've got to keep on trying if you really want to blah blah blah.

Talk about boring! But the thing is, I knew that Dad was right. I knew that I couldn't give up and that I've got to keep on trying. It's the only way I'm ever going to get an electric guitar for my birthday!

There was only one thing for it. I had to go and see Nigel again. And now I had the perfect excuse. I needed to take back his Radiohead CD!

When I got round to the house, Steven came to the door. He didn't seem very happy to see me. Mind you, I don't blame him. I think he knew I was only there to see Nigel again.

Then Colin came downstairs. He looked at the CD I was holding and said "Ah, Radiohead! Saw them at **Glastonbury** in 2003! They were fantastic!"

I had no idea where or what Glastonbury was, so Colin told me. He said it was this huge outdoor music festival that's held once a year on a farm in Somerset, in the south-west of England. It's on for three days and everyone camps there! You get to see loads and loads of different bands. In 2003 Colin saw **R.E.M**, **The Manic Street Preachers**, **The Kings Of Leon**, **The Darkness** and **The Libertines**. As well as Radiohead of course! It sounds brilliant! Next year he's going to take Nigel!

Some news just in! Colin is The Coolest Dad In The World! Not like *some* dads I know around here!

I went upstairs and knocked on Nigel's door. Nigel shouted for me to come in, so I did. He was lying on the floor, listening to music and flicking through a great big pile of magazines. The magazines were all about music and bands and stuff. There must have been at least a hundred of them! They looked great.

Nigel said that quite often you get a free **compilation CD** with a music magazine. A compilation is like, loads of different tracks by loads of different bands. I asked Nigel if he knew any bands from Manchester. Without even thinking Nigel said **Oasis**. (I told you Nigel knows everything about rock, didn't I?)

Oasis have got two brothers in them as well. Just like Radiohead! Their names are **Noel** and **Liam Gallagher**. Noel's the eldest. He plays guitar and writes most of the songs. Liam's the youngest. He's the lead singer and plays the tambourine. I think even I could play the tambourine! Yeah, and I might have to if I don't hurry up and solve these clues. Because I won't be getting a guitar at this rate, will I?

One of Nigel's magazines had a picture of the Gallagher brothers on the cover. I tried to think if they looked like anyone in our family, but they didn't. They had dark hair and eyebrows that almost met in the middle. There's no one in our family who looks like that! And the clue said something about cousins.

I asked Nigel if he knew any more bands from Manchester. He said hang on and started looking at the magazines again. After a few minutes he found one with another band on the cover. They were called **The Stone Roses**. Nigel said they were really popular in the late 1980s and early 90s. The magazine had loads of stuff about other bands from Manchester. They had names like **The Happy Mondays**, **The Inspiral Carpets** and **New Order**. And guess what?

They didn't call it Manchester, they called it *Mad*chester! I know! Weird or what?

Just before I left, Nigel gave me one of the compilation CDs! Not to borrow! To keep! He said it didn't matter because he'd got millions of them. I was dead pleased. But not as pleased as I was when I got home and looked at it!

Guess what one of the tracks was called? It was called This Charming Man! And guess what the name of the band was? They were called The Smiths! And what's my name? Darren Smith!

Do you see?

"Could this charming band from Manchester be distant cousins?" It could only be The Smiths! I didn't know for sure that they were from Manchester. But two minutes and a quick search on the internet later, I did!

Two clues down – one to go!

Some stuff about The Smiths

The Smiths formed in 1983 and split up in 1987. The line-up was **Morrissey** - vocals, **Johnny Marr** - guitar, **Andy Rourke** - bass, **Mike Joyce** - drums.

Morrissey used to appear on stage wearing a fake hearing aid and glasses and waving a bunch of flowers around his head!

J.K. Rowling is a big fan of The Smiths. (Maybe that's why Harry Potter wears glasses!)

Songs by The Smiths often had very long titles, like **Heaven Knows I'm Miserable Now** and **Last Night I Dreamt That Somebody Loved Me**. (That's two different songs by the way, not just one really long one!)

Morrissey is a well known vegetarian. One of The Smiths albums was even called **Meat Is Murder**!

(Paul McCartney from *The Beatles* is another famous veggie rock star. His first wife, Linda, started the Linda McCartney range of vegetarian foods. I'd better not advertise in case I get into trouble. But her veggie sausages are great!)

Thursday 20th october

Had this really weird dream last night. I dreamt that I was on stage, playing guitar in front of thousands of people! Which was great! But guess what? I could only play one chord! D major! It was like my fingers were stuck onto the neck of the guitar with Superglue or something!

Yeah and things got even more weird when I woke up and went downstairs. The

last clue was there, waiting for me, on the table.

"Never a cross word from this old punk? Try looking closer to home!"

I must admit, I thought Dad had lost the plot completely. That's if Dad ever *had* the plot to begin with of course! Ha ha!

Anyway, Mum came over and sat with me. She must have seen that I was looking a bit puzzled. I showed her the clue. When she read it she just grinned. I knew she knew the answer. But she wouldn't tell me what it was! I begged her to but it was no good. Mum said that I had to solve the clues myself. She said that Dad would go up the wall if she helped me. I said that's because Dad's boring.

Mum just looked at me and told me that maybe Dad wasn't as boring as I thought. I said, oh yeah, why's that then? But all Mum said was, look in the loft.

Well, I didn't need to be told twice! I was back up those stairs like a shot! I got the long pole with the hook on the end and pulled open the loft trapdoor. Then I pulled down the metal ladder to get into the loft.

I felt dead excited. I'd never been allowed in the loft by myself before! It was dark and musty smelling. I felt around for the light switch and switched it on.

There, in the middle of the loft, was an old cardboard box. It was as if it had been put there on purpose. I went over to the box and looked at it. There was a sticker on top. It just said one word. *Punk!*

I opened the box. It was full of old records! I took one out and looked at the cover. It was called ... I'd better not say what it was called, because there was a rude word in the title! But it was by a band called **The Sex Pistols** (and it's OK to say *sex* because that's a proper word and not a swear word or anything). The songs were called things like **Pretty Vacant, Anarchy In The UK** and **God Save The Queen**. And the singer was a guy called **Johnny Rotten**.

Oh and guess what? A name had been written on the back of the record in black felt pen. And what do you think the name was? Trevor Smith!

I couldn't believe it! My dad was a punk rocker! Mum was right. Dad's not as boring as I thought he was!

I took another record out from the box and looked at it. It was by a band called **The Clash**. There were these skinny guys on the cover, just staring at the camera and looking mean and moody. I looked on the back. The singer was called **Joe Strummer**.

The next record I looked at was by a band called **The Damned**. One of them was called **Rat Scabies** and another, **Captain Sensible**! Then there was a record by a band called **Generation X**. Their singer was called **Billy Idol**!

It was starting to look like the first thing you needed to do, if you wanted to be in a punk band, was give yourself a silly name!

Then I found this other record. It was by
a band called *The Wasters*. I looked on the
back of the cover. There was a picture of
the band. They all had spiky hair and were
pulling stupid faces.

Then I looked at one of the guys again. I
thought, *Hang on, I know him.* And I did. In
fact I still do.

It was my dad!

Except he wasn't called Trevor Smith. He was called Des Troy! Do you get it? Des Troy? Destroy!

So not only was my dad a punk rocker, he was actually in a band too! A proper band! And they made a record and everything! It was incredible! And then I thought, *Yeah that's the clue! The last clue! I've worked it out.*

"Never a cross word from this old punk? Try looking closer to home!"

Some news just in! Colin is The *Second* Coolest Dad In The World!

My dad's first!

Friday 21st October

Hi. Sorry I didn't do a list, or a fact file or anything yesterday. I was in a state of shock! And I'm sorry but you won't be getting one today either. Want to know why? It's my birthday. And guess what I got?

An electric guitar!

It's a beauty! It's black and white and it's a Fender Stratocaster! Well, not a real

Fender. But it's *like* one. It's called a **copy**.
Anyway it's fantastic and I love it to bits! It
came with a little amplifier and everything.
Now all I've got to do is learn to play it!

Dad's going to show me a couple more
chords. He says he only knows a few. He
says you didn't need to know many chords
to play punk rock! I told him about Nigel
and how amazing he is on guitar. Dad said
he'd love to hear him play.

Hey, that's an idea! Maybe I'll ask Nigel to come round some time. If I get good at playing guitar we can form a band together! Yeah! And Steven can be the singer if he wants! I wonder what we could call ourselves?

I'd better start making a list!

AUTHOR FACT FILE
JONATHAN MERES

Name 3 of the best albums ever recorded ...

Drums and Wires by XTC

Steve McQueen by Prefab Sprout

Late Registration by Kanye West.

Music is ...

Necessary.

What song title best sums you up?

Well as far as I know there isn't a song called "Tall Skinny Bald Bloke" so "Paperback Writer" by the Beatles.

If you could only listen to one song for the rest of your life, which would it be?

A really really long one.

If you had to go on Stars in their Eyes, which star would you be?

Britney Spears.

ILLUSTRATOR FACT FILE
DANIEL POSTGATE

Name 3 of the best albums ever recorded ...

Into the Music by Van Morrison

Trout Mask Replica by Captain Beefheart

Hunky Dory by David Bowie.

Music is ...

Power, according to Richard Ashcroft.

What song title best sums you up?

Shine on You Crazy Diamond by Pink Floyd.

If you could only listen to one song for the rest of your life, which would it be?

Heroes by David Bowie

If you had to go on Stars in their Eyes, which star would you be?

Frank Sinatra – I can do a good impression!

Barrington Stoke would like to thank all its readers for commenting on the manuscript before publication and in particular:

Scott Adam	Amy Jacob
Jake Barnes	Ashley Mackie
Amy Barton	Michael Murray
David Brett	Suzanne Prescott
Darren Clark	Duncan Ratcliffe
Kyle Connor	Josh Reid
Colin Duff	Aaron Roskilly
Kirsten Duffy	Brad Sewell
Amy Glynn	Shauna Sims
Craig Gorman	Alistair Waterson
Stephen Graham	Alex West
Cameron Greenlees	

Become a Consultant!

Would you like to give us feedback on our titles before they are published? Contact us at the email address below – we'd love to hear from you!

info@barringtonstoke.co.uk
www.barringtonstoke.co.uk

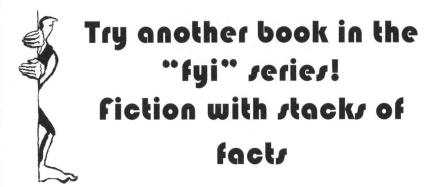

Try another book in the "fyi" series! Fiction with stacks of facts

The Egyptians
The Three-Legged Mummy by Vivian French

Boxing
The Greatest by Alan Gibbons

Scottish History and Literature
Dead Man's Close by Catherine MacPhail

All available from our website:
www.barringtonstoke.co.uk